I0663175

The Dream of a Ridiculous Man

A Philosophical Tale of Despair, Revelation, and Redemption

A Modern Translation

Adapted for the Contemporary Reader

Fyodor Dostoevsky

Translated by Tim Zengerink

Table of Contents

Preface - Message to the Reader

What If You Could Help Rebuild the Greatest Library in Human History?

Thousands of years ago, the Library of Alexandria stood as the crown jewel of human achievement — a sanctuary where the collected wisdom of every known civilization was gathered, preserved, and shared freely.

And then, it was lost.

Through fire, conquest, and the slow erosion of time, humanity lost not just books — but ideas, dreams, discoveries, and stories that could have changed the world forever.

Today, the Library of Alexandria lives again — and you are invited to be a part of its restoration.

Our mission is simple yet profound:

To rebuild the greatest library the world has ever known, and to translate all timeless works into every language and dialect, so that no seeker of knowledge is ever left behind again.

By joining our movement to rebuild the modern Library of Alexandria, you become part of an unprecedented mission:

- **Unlimited Access to the Greatest Audiobooks & eBooks Ever Written:**

  Instantly explore thousands of legendary works—Plato, Shakespeare, Jane Austen, Leo Tolstoy, and countless more. All instantly available to read or listen, placing a complete literary universe at your fingertips.

- **Beautiful Paperback & Deluxe Editions at Printing Cost**

  Own any title as an elegant paperback, deluxe hardcover, or stunning collectible boxset—offered to you at true printing cost, delivered straight to your door. Build your personal Library of Alexandria, crafted for beauty, built for durability, and worthy of proud display.

- **Fresh Translations for Modern Readers—in Every Language & Dialect**

  Enjoy timeless masterpieces reimagined in clear, contemporary language—no more outdated phrases or obscure references. Alongside the original versions, we're tirelessly translating these classics into every language and dialect imaginable, ensuring accessibility and understanding across cultures and generations.

- **Join a Global Renaissance of Literature & Knowledge**

  You directly support expanding our library, publishing deluxe editions at true cost, translating works into all global languages, and bringing humanity's greatest stories to people everywhere. By joining today, you're not just preserving a legacy of masterpieces; you set in motion a powerful wave of literary accessibility.

Become a Torchbearer of Knowledge.

Join us for free now at **LibraryofAlexandria.com**

Together, we will ensure that the light of human wisdom never fades again.

With gratitude and a shared love of knowledge,

The Modern Library of Alexandria Team

Visit:

www.libraryofalexandria.com

Or scan the code below:

Chapter I

I'm a ridiculous person. People now say I'm crazy. Honestly, that would feel like a promotion—if they didn't still think I'm just as silly as before. But now, I don't mind anymore. In fact, I care about them all deeply, even when they laugh at me. Actually, especially when they laugh at me, I feel closer to them. I could laugh along with them—not because I'm laughing at myself, but because I care about them. Still, it makes me sad. Sad because they don't know the truth… and I do. And it's so hard being the only one who knows. But they'll never get that. No, they never will.

When I was younger, it hurt to feel like a joke. And it wasn't just in my head—I really was ridiculous. I've known it for most of my life. I think I realized it when I was seven. I went to school, then to college, and the more I studied, the more I felt like everything I learned just proved how foolish I was. It felt like all of school existed just to remind me I was a joke.

Life outside school was no better. Year after year, I became more aware of how silly I must seem. People laughed at me all the time. But what they didn't know was that no one understood how ridiculous I was better than I did. That was the worst part—they laughed, not knowing I was already fully aware. And it was my pride that kept me from telling them. That pride only grew stronger as I got older. If I had ever admitted it out loud, I think I would have ended my life that same night.

As a teenager, I was terrified I'd slip up and say something. But when I became an adult, I slowly became calmer, though I still knew how absurd I was. I don't know why it changed. Maybe it was because something even heavier started to grow inside me. I began to believe that nothing really mattered.

I had felt it for a while, but last year it hit me completely. It suddenly didn't matter to me if the world existed or not. It made no difference. At first, I thought maybe things had mattered in the past. But later, I realized maybe the past was an illusion too. Little by little, I started to believe the future didn't matter either. After that, I stopped being angry at people. I barely noticed them anymore.

It started to show in little ways. I would bump into people on the street—not because I was lost in thought, but because I just didn't care. I wasn't thinking at all anymore. Nothing meant anything. I hadn't solved a single one of my many questions. But I didn't care about the answers anymore. Eventually, even the questions faded away. And that's when I discovered the truth.

I found out the truth last November—on the third, to be exact—and I remember every moment since. That evening was one of the darkest and gloomiest I've ever seen. I was walking home around eleven. It had rained all day—a cold, angry kind of rain that felt like it hated everyone. It finally stopped around ten, but what followed was worse: thick, wet air rising off every street and building like steam.

I remember thinking the streetlights made everything feel even sadder. If they'd just turned off the lights, maybe the darkness wouldn't feel so hopeless. I hadn't eaten much that day. I'd been with an engineer and two other friends that evening. They got all worked up about something, but I could tell they didn't truly care. They were just pretending. Eventually, I told them.

"My friends," I said, "you don't really care about any of this." They didn't get upset—they just laughed at me. I wasn't mad; I just didn't care anymore, and they could see it. That's why it made them laugh.

As I walked home, still thinking about those streetlights, I looked up at the sky. It was cloudy and dark, but there were gaps where the sky peeked through—deep black spots. In one of those gaps, I saw a star. I stared at it. That star sparked something in me: I decided I would finally kill myself that night.

I had decided to do it two months earlier. Even though I had little money, I saved up and bought a good revolver and loaded it the day I brought it home. But for two months, I hadn't used it. It just stayed in my drawer. I was waiting for the right moment—waiting until I felt something. I don't know why. Every night I came home thinking, "Tonight's the night." But it never was. Then I saw that star, and it gave me the push I needed. That night would be the night.

While I was still staring at the sky, a little girl grabbed my arm. The street was almost empty. I remember seeing a cab driver asleep in his cab nearby. The girl looked about eight. She wore a thin, soaked dress and a scarf over her head. Her shoes were torn and soaked through—I can still picture them clearly. She tugged on my sleeve and started crying out. She wasn't sobbing like a baby, but gasping and trembling, barely able to speak because she was so cold and scared. She kept crying, "Mommy, mommy!"

I turned to look at her but didn't say anything. Then I kept walking. But she followed me, still pulling on me. Her voice had that desperate sound only terrified children have. Even though she couldn't say exactly what was wrong, I understood her mom was in serious trouble—maybe dying—and the girl had run out into the night to find someone, anyone, who could help.

Still, I didn't go with her. I wanted her to leave. I told her to find a police officer. But she kept running beside me, crying and begging. Eventually, I snapped. I stomped my foot and yelled at her. She shouted, "Please, sir!"—but then she suddenly ran off, crossing the street toward someone else.

I climbed up to my fifth-floor room. I rent a small place in a building with other tenants. My room has a curved attic window, a beat-up leather couch, a table with some books, two chairs, and an old armchair that's worn out but comfortable. I lit a candle and sat down to think.

Next door, I could hear chaos again. It had been like that for three days straight. A retired army captain lived there with some shady friends. They drank vodka and played cards all night. The night before, there had even been a fight—I heard two of them dragging each other across the floor by the hair. The landlady wanted to complain, but she was too scared.

Another tenant was a sickly woman with three small kids. They were terrified of the noise. They lay awake all night, praying and trembling. One of the kids even had a seizure from the stress. I'd also heard the captain begged strangers for money on the street. No one would hire him. But weirdly, none of this bothered me. I didn't even hear the shouting anymore. I avoided him, and he avoided me. And still, every night I stayed up in my chair, doing nothing. I didn't care, didn't think. I just sat there. I only read during the daytime.

Every night, I burned through an entire candle. I just sat there quietly. That night, I took out the revolver and placed it on the table. I looked at it and asked myself, "Is this really it?" Then I answered, completely sure, "Yes. This is it." I knew I was going to do it that night. I just didn't know how long I'd sit there first.

And I would have done it—if that little girl hadn't stopped me.

Chapter II

Even though nothing really mattered to me anymore, I could still feel things—like pain. If someone hit me, it would hurt. And emotionally, it was the same. If something sad happened, I would still feel sympathy, just like I used to back when life seemed to matter. That night, I did feel sympathy. I would've normally helped a child without hesitation. So why didn't I help that little girl?

Because in that moment, a strange thought popped into my head. While she was tugging at me and calling for help, I suddenly had a question I couldn't answer. It wasn't even a deep question—it just annoyed me. I was bothered by the idea that if I was really planning to end my life that night, then nothing in the world should have mattered to me anymore. So why did I feel sad for that girl? Why did I care at all? I remember feeling sorry for her—deeply sorry, even. It didn't make sense, and it didn't match the way I thought I was supposed to feel. But that feeling stayed with me when I got home and sat down at my table. I became more upset than I had been in a long time.

Thought after thought filled my mind. I realized that as long as I was still alive, I could still feel things—pain, anger, guilt. So fine. But if I was going to kill myself in, say, two hours, why should that girl matter to me? Why should I care about shame or anything else in the world? Soon I'd be nothing at all—just gone.

And if I was really going to stop existing, if the whole world would disappear for me the moment I died, then why did I still feel bad about yelling at a child? Why did I feel ashamed of acting cruel? I had stomped and shouted at that scared little girl as if to prove, "I don't care. I can act heartless if I want. I'm going to be gone soon anyway."

Do you think that's why I yelled at her? I think so now. I acted like I had the freedom to be cruel because I thought nothing mattered anymore. But deep down, I started to feel like everything somehow did depend on me. It felt like the world existed just for me—and that if I died, then for me, at least, the world would end too. Maybe the whole world is only real because I'm here to see it. Maybe all of it—everything and everyone—is just a part of me.

I sat there, spinning in new thoughts. One weird idea followed another. At one point, I imagined that if I had once lived on another planet—like the moon or

Mars—and had done something terribly shameful there, something so awful I couldn't even describe it… and if I came to Earth afterward and remembered that shame, but knew I'd never go back—would I still feel guilty about what I did?

These were strange, useless questions—especially with the revolver lying in front of me. I knew deep down I was still going to pull the trigger. But those thoughts got to me. They stirred something inside. I couldn't die yet—not until I figured some of it out.

So, in a strange way, that child saved me. Because of her, I delayed pulling the trigger. I stayed in my chair, stuck in thought, while next door the noise from the captain's room finally began to quiet down. They had stopped their card game and were falling asleep, still arguing a bit but growing tired.

And then, something unexpected happened. I fell asleep. Right there, in my chair at the table. I didn't even notice it happening—it just did. That had never happened to me before.

Dreams are strange. Some parts are incredibly clear, filled with tiny details like carefully made jewelry. Other parts rush by so quickly that you barely notice them— like traveling through space or time without even realizing it. Dreams don't follow logic—they follow feelings. And yet, sometimes your brain does things in dreams that are more complicated than anything you'd ever think of while awake.

For example, my brother died five years ago. But I still dream about him sometimes. In the dream, he's alive and involved in my life, and we're doing things together. And even though I know in the dream that he's dead, I'm not surprised to see him. My brain just accepts it. That's the strange thing about dreams.

Anyway, let me get to the dream I had that night—on the third of November. People now tell me it was "just a dream," like it doesn't matter. But why should it matter whether it was real or not? If the dream showed me the truth, then it was real in the only way that counts. Because once you've seen the truth—really seen it—you know it's the truth. There's no going back. It doesn't matter whether you were awake or asleep when you learned it.

So yes, it was a dream—but that dream saved me. It gave me a new life—strong, full of meaning, and completely different from the one I was about to throw away.

Let me tell you what I dreamed.

Chapter III

I mentioned earlier that I fell asleep without meaning to, and even in my sleep, I felt like I was still thinking about the same things. In my dream, I suddenly saw myself picking up the revolver and aiming it—not at my head like I had planned, but right at my heart. I had always planned to aim at my right temple, but in the dream, I pointed it at my chest. I waited a moment. Then the candle, the table, and the wall in front of me all started to shake and shift. I quickly pulled the trigger.

In dreams, you might fall or get hurt, but you usually don't feel pain—unless you actually bump into something in real life while sleeping. That's how it was for me. I didn't feel pain, but it was like something inside me had been shaken, like everything suddenly faded away and turned pitch black. I felt like I was blind and numb, lying flat on my back on something hard. I couldn't move or see anything. I heard voices—people yelling, the captain shouting, the landlady screaming. Then everything changed again.

Now I was in a closed coffin. I could feel it shaking as people carried it. And then, for the first time, the thought hit me: I was dead. Completely dead. I had no doubt about it. I couldn't see or move, but I was still thinking and feeling. But soon, just like in most dreams, I accepted it without questioning. I didn't panic. I just accepted that I was dead.

Then I was buried. Everyone left, and I was alone. Completely alone. I couldn't move, but strangely, I didn't expect anything either. I simply accepted that a dead person has nothing to expect. It was cold, especially in my feet. That's what I always imagined the grave would feel like—cold and damp. And now I was really feeling it.

I don't know how much time passed—maybe an hour, maybe days. But then, all of a sudden, I felt a drop of water fall on my closed left eye. It must've leaked through the coffin lid. Then a minute later, another drop fell. Then another, every minute, one after the other. Slowly, something started to stir inside me—deep frustration, and even a bit of pain. "That's where I was shot," I thought. "That's the bullet wound."

And still, drop by drop, the water kept falling on my eye. Suddenly, with my whole being—not with a voice—I called out to whatever force was behind this.

"Whoever you are, if you really exist, and if something more reasonable than this is possible, then let it happen now. But if this is your way of punishing

16

me for my stupid suicide—if this awful, senseless afterlife is your revenge—then just know this: no torture you give me will be worse than the quiet hatred I feel right now. I'll feel it forever, even if you make me suffer for a million years!"

I said that and went silent. A whole minute passed in stillness. Then another drop fell. But I suddenly knew, without any doubt at all, that something was about to change.

And just like that, my grave was torn open. I don't know if someone dug me up or if it just split open. But some dark, mysterious being lifted me out, and the next thing I knew, we were flying through space. Suddenly, I could see again. It was the middle of the night—and I had never seen a darkness so deep. We were flying far away from Earth. I didn't ask the being who carried me any questions. I felt proud. I told myself I wasn't afraid—and I was proud that I wasn't afraid.

I don't know how long we flew. Time didn't work the same way anymore, just like in most dreams. You skip past things like space and time, and only stop at moments that your heart needs to feel. Suddenly, I saw a star in the darkness.

"Is that Sirius?" I asked without meaning to.

"No," the being answered. "That's the star you saw between the clouds when you were walking home."

Its face looked somewhat human. Strangely, I didn't like this creature at all. I actually felt disgusted by it. I had expected nothingness—complete non-existence. That's why I had shot myself. But now I was in the hands of something that wasn't human but was still alive. "So there really is life after death," I thought to myself in a casual, dream-like way. But deep down, I still felt like myself. I thought, "If I have to exist again, controlled by some mysterious power, I won't let it crush me or break my pride."

Then I turned to the being and said, "You know I'm scared of you—and you look down on me because of it." I couldn't help but say it, even though it made me feel ashamed. The shame hit me like a stab in the heart.

The being didn't reply. But suddenly, I felt something even worse: not only did it not respect me—it was laughing at me. It didn't even pity me. And somehow I knew that wherever we were going, it had something to do with me—and me alone.

My fear grew stronger. The being didn't speak, but I could feel its message soaking into every part of me. We were flying through empty, endless space. I couldn't recognize any of the stars anymore. I knew there were stars so far away that their light takes thousands or even millions of years to reach Earth. Maybe we were flying through those regions now.

I felt something heavy in my heart, a horrible kind of dread. Then all of a sudden, I felt something familiar—something that touched my soul deeply. I saw a sun. Not our sun, I knew that. We were far, far away from Earth. But somehow I just knew it was a sun exactly like ours. A copy of it.

And then something inside me lit up. The light of that sun reminded me of the sun I once knew. It stirred something in me—something old and warm. For the first time since I had been buried, I felt alive again. Really alive.

"But if that's really the sun," I said, "and it's just like our sun—then where's Earth?"

My guide pointed to a far-off star, glowing with a green light. We were flying straight toward it.

"Wait," I said, "does that mean the universe repeats itself? Is that the rule of nature? And if that planet is another Earth… is it exactly like ours? Is it just as poor and broken, just as full of sorrow—but still loved forever, even by those who didn't appreciate it? Can it inspire the same deep love that we feel for our own world?"

As I said this, a powerful wave of love swept over me—for the Earth I had left behind. I suddenly thought of the little girl I had ignored.

"You'll see it all," my guide replied, but there was sadness in his voice.

We were getting closer to the planet. It grew larger before my eyes. I could make out the oceans, and even the shape of Europe. Suddenly, a strong feeling of jealousy burned inside me.

"How can there be another Earth?" I said. "And what's the point? I can only love the Earth I left behind—the one I stained with my own blood when I shot myself. Even then, in my worst moment, I still loved it. Maybe that night, I loved it more than ever before."

"Is there pain on this new Earth?" I asked. "On our Earth, we only know how to love through pain. That's the only kind of love we understand. I need that kind of love. I long for it. Right now, I want to fall to the ground and kiss the Earth I left behind with tears in my eyes. I don't want any other life. I won't accept life on a different Earth!"

But then I noticed my guide was gone.

Suddenly—and I don't know how it happened—I found myself standing on this new Earth, in the middle of a bright, sunny day. It was as beautiful as paradise. I think I was on one of the Greek islands, or maybe the coast nearby.

Everything looked the same as on our Earth, but somehow it all felt more alive, more joyful—like the whole world was celebrating something sacred. The sea, green like emerald, gently splashed onto the shore, like it was softly kissing it. The tall trees stood proudly in full bloom. Their countless leaves swayed and whispered to me, like they were saying words of love. The grass glowed with bright, sweet-smelling flowers.

Birds flew in flocks above me. Some landed on my shoulders and arms, flapping their wings happily, like they were greeting an old friend.

Then I saw the people who lived there. They came toward me, smiling, surrounding me. They kissed me and welcomed me. They were like children of the sun—children of their sun. And they were beautiful. I had never seen people so beautiful. Maybe you could find a small glimpse of it in our own world, in the faces of young children—but only a faint trace.

Their eyes were clear and bright. Their faces glowed with kindness, wisdom, and deep peace. They looked joyful and calm, like they truly understood everything. Their voices and laughter sounded innocent and full of pure happiness.

The moment I looked at them, I understood. I just knew. This was Earth before anything went wrong. These were people who had never sinned. They were living in the paradise that, according to old stories, our first ancestors once lived in before they lost it. The only difference was that here, all of Earth was that paradise.

They laughed with joy and crowded around me. They gently touched my face and welcomed me into their homes. No one asked any questions, but I felt like they already knew everything. They weren't trying to figure me out—they were simply trying to heal me. They wanted to take away the pain I carried.

Chapter IV

And you know what? Even if it really was just a dream, the feeling of love I felt from those kind, beautiful people has stayed with me forever. It still feels like their love is reaching out to me, even now. I saw them with my own eyes, I knew them, and I truly believed in them. I loved them—and later, I suffered because of what happened to them.

Even during the dream, I realized there were many things I didn't understand about them. As a modern Russian, raised with science and reason, I couldn't figure out how they could know so much without having anything like our scientific knowledge. But I quickly saw that their understanding came from a different place than ours. Their hopes and goals weren't like ours at all. They didn't chase knowledge the way we do, because their lives were already full and meaningful.

Their understanding was much deeper than ours. We study science to try and explain what life is and how people should live—but they didn't need science to live well. They already knew how to live. I could tell they had a higher kind of wisdom, even though I couldn't understand it myself.

They showed me their trees, and I was amazed at how deeply they loved them. It was like the trees were friends to them—like they were actually talking to them. And honestly, I think they really were communicating. They had found a way to speak with nature, and the trees understood. They looked at everything that way— even animals. The animals didn't fear them. They lived together peacefully because the animals could feel their love.

They pointed to the stars and told me something about them too—something I couldn't fully grasp. But I felt sure they were connected to the stars, not just through thoughts, but through some living bond. They never tried to force me to understand any of it. They loved me even though I didn't understand. And I knew they'd never fully understand me. That's why I rarely spoke about our Earth.

Instead, I kissed the ground they walked on and silently admired them. They let me do this without embarrassment. They weren't proud or shy about it— they just loved deeply and purely. When I sometimes dropped to my knees and kissed their feet with tears in my eyes, they didn't feel sorry for me. They knew I was expressing love, and they returned it with joy.

I kept wondering how it was possible that they never once offended me or made me feel jealous. Even though I had always been someone who liked to show off and exaggerate, I never once felt the urge to impress them. I didn't try to share what I knew—even though they probably didn't know anything about it—because I didn't feel the need.

They were cheerful, playful, and gentle like children. They walked through their forests and meadows, singing sweet songs. Their food was simple—fruit from trees, honey from the woods, milk from animals who loved them back. They did some work to get food and clothes, but it was easy and not tiring.

They loved each other and had children, but there was none of that dark, selfish desire that you often see in people on our Earth. That kind of desire that leads to pain and sin—it didn't exist there. When children were born, they welcomed them with happiness—as if they were welcoming new people into their joy.

There was no arguing, no jealousy. They didn't even know what those words meant. Their children belonged to everyone, because they all lived like one big family. Illness was rare, though death still came. But even death wasn't frightening. The elderly passed away peacefully, like falling asleep, surrounded by loved ones who smiled and gave their blessings. I never saw sadness or tears—only a kind of peaceful joy, a quiet celebration of love.

It even seemed like death didn't really separate them. They still felt connected to those who had passed on. When I asked them about immortality, they didn't quite understand the question. But I could tell they knew it existed—not through logic, but through something deeper. It wasn't a debate for them. It was just part of life.

They had no churches or temples, but they lived in constant connection with the universe. They had no official religion, but they believed that once their earthly happiness reached its limit, something even greater would come—a deeper connection with everything. They looked forward to it calmly, without longing or fear, because they already carried a bit of that future joy inside them.

At night, before sleeping, they sang together in beautiful harmony. Their songs expressed everything they had felt during the day—the joy, the beauty, the peace. They sang about nature, the sea, the forests. They made up songs for each other too, praising one another like children do. The songs were simple, but they were full of love. They didn't just sing—they admired and appreciated each other constantly.

Some of their songs were so deep and powerful that I couldn't really understand them. I knew the words, but the meaning was beyond me. Still, my heart soaked it in without needing to analyze.

I told them once that I had sensed their world long before I ever saw it. That on our Earth, I had sometimes felt a painful longing for something beautiful and far away. That when I watched the sun set, I would cry without knowing why. That even when I hated people, I couldn't help loving them too—and that my love was always filled with sorrow. Why couldn't I love them without feeling pain? Why couldn't I hate them without also feeling love?

They listened quietly. I don't think they fully understood what I meant, but I know they felt the pain in my voice. They saw how deeply I longed for the people I had left behind. And when they looked at me with those gentle, loving eyes, I felt my heart becoming pure again—like theirs. That feeling of life, that fullness, was so strong it took my breath away. I worshiped them silently.

Now, everyone laughs at me. They say no one dreams with that much detail. They tell me I just felt one strong emotion in the dream and made up all the rest after I woke up. And maybe they're right. When I said maybe it was just a dream, they laughed even harder.

Yes, maybe all I remembered was the emotion—that deep, aching love. And maybe the actual images and moments in the dream got blurry when I woke up, so I had to fill in the missing parts on my own. Maybe I added details because I wanted so badly to share it, to make others understand. Maybe that messed it up.

But still—how could I not believe it was real? Maybe it was a thousand times more beautiful and joyful than I can even describe. Even if it was a dream, it felt real.

Want to hear a secret? Maybe it wasn't a dream at all. Because what happened next—what happened after—was so awful, so painfully true, that there's no way I could have made it up. My heart might've created the dream, but could my heart alone have imagined what came next? Could my small, selfish mind have come up with such a deep truth?

I'll tell you now, something I've been hiding.

The truth is… I ruined it all. I corrupted them.

Chapter V

Yes, it's true—I ended up ruining everything. I don't know how it happened, but I remember it clearly. The dream covered thousands of years, but what stayed with me was the feeling of what I had done. Somehow, I was the reason they lost their innocence.

Like a deadly virus, like a tiny seed of poison, I infected that perfect world—so peaceful and pure before I arrived. They learned how to lie. At first, it seemed harmless—maybe just a joke, a playful look, a tiny act of flirtation. But that small seed of dishonesty crept into their hearts, and they liked it.

Soon desire took root. Then came jealousy. And then, cruelty.

I don't remember everything clearly, but it didn't take long before the first person was killed. They were shocked, even horrified—but from that moment on, things began to fall apart. They formed groups and turned against one another. They blamed and accused. They learned what shame was, and shame led them to chase after something they called virtue.

They invented the idea of honor. Every group made flags and stood behind them. They began to hurt animals, and the animals, once loving, ran away and turned wild. The people fought to separate themselves. They claimed what was "mine" and "yours." They began to speak different languages.

They learned sorrow—and even started to love it. They believed that only by suffering could they find truth.

Then science was born. As they grew more wicked, they began to speak about brotherhood and kindness—but only because they understood how broken they had become. They made laws to try to fix themselves. They spoke of justice and built whole systems to enforce it—complete with executions.

They forgot what they had lost. Some even refused to believe they'd ever been happy or innocent. They laughed at the idea, called it a myth or a dream. They couldn't even picture what happiness looked like anymore. But strangely, even though they stopped believing in it, they still wanted it—so badly, like children.

They made an idol out of their own wish to be happy again. They built temples to that idea and worshipped it—crying as they prayed to something they thought they could never reach again. And yet, if someone had shown them the way back to that lost innocence and asked, "Do you want to return?"—they would've said no.

They told me:

"Yes, we lie and do wrong. We know it. We're ashamed and we suffer. We punish ourselves more than any God could. But we have science, and with it, we'll find the truth. And we'll reach it on our own. Learning is better than feeling. Being aware of life is more important than life itself. Science will give us wisdom, and wisdom will teach us the rules of happiness—and those rules are greater than happiness itself."

That's what they believed. And once they started believing that, everyone began loving themselves more than anyone else. They became so obsessed with protecting their personal rights that they crushed those rights in others just to keep their own.

Slavery came back, even willing slavery. The weak gave themselves to the strong in exchange for power over the even weaker.

Holy people came and warned them—begged them to see how far they had fallen, how proud they had become, how they had lost all sense of balance. These prophets were mocked or stoned to death. Sacred blood was spilled at the doors of their temples.

Then came others who tried to bring everyone back together. They wanted a world where people could still love themselves most, but without harming others. They hoped for peace and unity. But instead of peace, new wars broke out—wars over these very ideas.

Each side believed wisdom and science would eventually bring harmony. And to speed up the process, the "wise" started killing off everyone who didn't understand them—so their new world wouldn't be delayed.

But the will to survive grew weaker. A new kind of person appeared—selfish, proud, and greedy. They wanted everything. If they couldn't have it, they chose crime... or death.

New religions were born—ones that worshipped nonexistence, that believed the greatest peace came through destruction. People got tired of their endless struggles. You could see the pain on their faces.

And then they began to say, "Suffering is beautiful." They sang songs that praised pain.

I walked among them, crying, reaching out my hands. I wept for them. And strangely, I loved them more than ever—more than when they were innocent.

I loved the broken Earth they had made, even more than the perfect one I had first seen—because now it held sorrow.

I had always loved sadness—but only for myself. Now I cried for them.

I begged them to forgive me. I told them it was all my fault. I had brought them lies, corruption, and pain. I begged them to crucify me. I even showed them how to build a cross.

I couldn't kill myself. I didn't have the strength. But I wanted to suffer. I wanted them to make me bleed for what I had done. I wanted them to drain my life away in agony.

But they just laughed.

They called me crazy. Eventually, they said I was dangerous. They warned me that if I didn't stop talking, they would lock me in an asylum.

Then an unbearable sorrow filled my soul. My heart felt like it was breaking. I thought I was dying.

And then…

I woke up.

***

It was early morning—about six o'clock, just before sunrise. I woke up in my usual armchair. The candle had burned out, and everything was quiet. Even the captain's room, which was usually noisy, was completely still. That never happened before. I stood up, confused and surprised, because I had never fallen asleep like that in the chair—not even once.

As I stood there getting my thoughts together, I noticed the loaded revolver still lying on the table. I quickly shoved it away. Suddenly, I felt overwhelmed with emotion. "Life!" I cried silently. "Life!" I lifted my hands and began to cry—not with words, but with tears. A huge wave of joy and peace filled my heart. I knew then that I had to share what I had seen. I had to tell people the truth. I made up my mind in that moment to devote the rest of my life to that mission. I was going to tell the world what I had seen with my own eyes.

Since then, I've been trying to spread the message. I even love the people who laugh at me more than the ones who don't. I don't know why—it just feels that way.

People say I talk in a confused way, and it's true. If I'm this confused now, what will I be like later on? I'll probably make a lot of mistakes before I figure out how to explain everything—how to say it the right way, how to do the right things. It's not easy. But everyone makes mistakes. And even though people take different paths—whether they're saints or criminals—we're all searching for the same thing.

Here's what's new, though: I can't be completely wrong. I've seen the truth. I've seen it, and now I know that people can be kind and happy while still living on this earth. I just can't believe that evil is normal for humans. That's the belief everyone laughs at, but I can't stop believing it. I didn't just make it up in my head—I saw it. The image of what I saw lives inside me, and I know it's possible for people to live that way.

Sure, I'll make some mistakes. I might even repeat what others have said before. But that image will always be with me, guiding me and reminding me of what I saw. I feel strong and full of energy, and I'll keep going— even if it takes a thousand years.

At first, I thought about hiding the fact that I was the one who ruined everything in my dream. But that was a mistake—my first mistake. The truth whispered to me, reminded me not to lie, and helped me fix it.

Still, I don't know how to create a paradise on earth. I saw it, but I don't know how to explain it. Since that dream, I've lost the words to describe it—especially the most important ones. But that's okay. I'll keep going and keep talking. I won't stop, because I know what I saw, even if I can't explain it.

The people who mock me don't understand that. "It was just a dream," they say. "It was a hallucination." But so what? Why do they think that matters? And they say it with such pride. Just a dream? Isn't life itself kind of like a dream?

And even if that paradise never actually happens, I'll keep preaching about it. Because it's really so simple— everything could change in one day, in just one hour. The key is this: love others the way you love yourself. That's it. That's all we need. Once we do that, everything else will fall into place.

People have said it a million times. But we've never truly lived by it. People think knowing how to live is more important than just living. They think understanding happiness is better than actually being happy. That's what we're up against—and I'm ready to fight it.

If everyone truly wanted it, everything could change right now.

***

And I found that little girl again... and I won't stop—I'll keep going, no matter what!

The End

Thank You for Reading

Dear Reader,

We hope this timeless classic has sparked your imagination and enriched your literary journey. Now that you've turned the final page, we want to share a vision for the future of reading—one where every classic you've ever wanted to explore is at your fingertips, in a format that best suits your life.

We'd like to invite you to gain immediate, unlimited digital & audiobook access to hundreds of the most treasured literary classics ever written—along with the option to secure deluxe paperback, hardcover & box set editions at printing cost. Together, we can spark a new global literary renaissance alongside our small, independent publishing house called "The Library of Alexandria."

Thousands of years ago, the Library of Alexandria stood as a beacon of knowledge—until it was lost to history. We aim to reignite that spirit of preservation and discovery right now, in the modern age—only this time, it's accessible to all, in every language and every format.

Picture a world where every timeless classic, novel, poem, or philosophical treatise is not only available to read but also updated for today's readers—modernized, translated into any language or dialect, and ready to enjoy in any format you choose, whether that is in an eBook, audiobook, paperback, or deluxe hardcover & box set version a printing cost.

By joining our movement to rebuild the modern Library of Alexandria, you become part of an unprecedented mission to offer:

- **Unlimited Audiobook & eBook Access to the Greatest Classics of All Time**

  Instantly explore thousands of legendary works, from Plato and Shakespeare to Jane Austen and Leo Tolstoy. All are instantly ready to read or listen to, giving you a complete literary universe at your fingertips.

- **Paperback & Deluxe Editions at Printing Costs:**

  Purchase any title in a paperback, deluxe hardbound, or deluxe boxset edition at printing costs, shipped right to your doorstep. Curate your personal library of Alexandria with editions worthy of display—crafted to last, designed to captivate, and delivered straight to your door.

- **Modern translations for Contemporary Readers in all languages and dialects**

  Discover a vast selection of classics reimagined in clear, current language—no more struggling with outdated phrases or obscure references. Next to the original versions, we aim to offer translations in as many languages and dialects as possible.

  As we continue our translation efforts and add new languages, readers everywhere can connect with these works as if they were written today. By bridging linguistic divides, you're contributing to ensuring that these timeless stories become more meaningful, accessible, and inspiring for people across the globe.

- **Your Personal Library of Alexandria:**

  Over the months and years, you'll curate a unique physical archive of classics—each volume a testament to your taste, curiosity, and love of knowledge. It's not just about owning books—it's about curating a cultural legacy you'll cherish and pass down for generations to come.

- **Join a Global Literary Renaissance:**

  Your support fuels an ongoing mission: allowing us to reinvest in offering deluxe print editions (including special boxsets) at their true cost, broaden the range of available formats and translations, and extend the reach of these works to new audiences worldwide. By joining today, you're not just preserving a legacy of masterpieces; you set in motion a powerful wave of literary accessibility.

We are more than a publisher—we're a movement, and we can't do it alone. Your support lets us scale our mission, preserving and reimagining history's greatest works for tomorrow's readers.

Become a Torchbearer of knowledge.

Thank you for picking up this book and allowing us into your literary journey. As you turn the pages, know that you're part of something larger: a global effort to keep these stories alive, share their wisdom across borders and generations, and spark a true cultural revival for the modern era.

If this resonates with you—please consider taking the next step by visiting:

www.libraryofalexandria.com

With gratitude and a shared love of knowledge,

The Modern Library of Alexandria Team

Visit:

www.libraryofalexandria.com

Or scan the code below:

www.ingramcontent.com/pod-product-compliance
Lightning Source LLC
Chambersburg PA
CBHW011526240626
47154CB00009B/2987